THIS NOVELETTE IS AN EXCERPT FROM
THE DIFFERENT KINDS OF MONSTERS,
BY SETH CHAMBERS

Seth can be contacted directly at
SethChambersAuthor@gmail.com

OTHER WORKS
BY SETH CHAMBERS:

What Rough Beasts:
Twenty-Five Monstrous Tales

Beautiful Machines:
Tales Of The Uncanny

Little Bird:
A Novel Of Love & Transformation

We Happy Few

Her Rule Would Always Last

By Seth Chambers

1

For the first moments of her awareness, she struggled through the thin shell of her prison. During that brief time, she had no thoughts but freedom. When she finally succeeded, endorphins washed over neuroreceptors, and she gave forth a mighty roar, although to other ears it might've been a little squeak.

But the spirit was there.

She rested, tiny lungs fluttering like butterflies. Hatching is strenuous work; she needed to recover. Dark as it was in her underground nest, she sensed movement nearby: her nestlings, just starting their journeys to freedom.

In her wordless way, she felt a tingle of pride: she was First! And this is how she thought of herself: *First!*

Second was almost out of her shell. First rolled to her feet, not about to be overtaken by her sibling. The soil against her feet was a new sensation, followed by a medley of smells rushing through her nose, from her own body, her siblings, and Somewhere Beyond. Driven by eons of instinct, her brain circuits scrambled to make sense of it all.

Now Second was free of her shell. First breathed in her sibling's scent and heard her panting, as she had panted shortly before.

First took her first step. It was clumsy and awkward, but then again she was mere minutes from the egg. Her second step was marginally better. With her third step, she felt the floor of the nest slope upward. Instinctively, the baby allosaurus knew there was much to learn in a very short time.

With her fourth step, she toppled forward, so that her fore claws impacted the side of the nest. Meanwhile, her burgeoning sense of smell told her that Third was now breaking free of his egg.

First clawed her way upward, ragged breaths drawing damp soil into her mouth, her feet bearing into loose dirt, her thighs burning with strain. This went on for a long time. In fact, at one point the majority of her young life was spent in this climb to the top of the underground nest.

It wasn't until she was close to blacking out from exertion that her reward finally came: a single, blinding sliver of light. Until this moment, she had no concept of sight. She screeched (no mighty roar this time), and tumbled back down the side of her nest, gasping.

By the time Last finally emerged from his shell, First had already lived an eventful life.

2

First peered at the sliver of light streaming in from the top of the nest, where she had managed to break through. As she watched, something massive pushed through the roof. More light poured in. After her eyes adjusted, she beheld a head, larger than herself and her nestlings combined. The maw opened, revealing long rows of serrated teeth.

First and her nestlings cowered at the bottom of the nest, tiny bodies shivering. The monstrous head loomed in close enough for the hot breath wash over them. Then First sucked in the scent and her muscles relaxed.

Mother.

Protector.

Her siblings also sniffed and relaxed.

Then Mother drew a rushing intake of air through her great nostrils as she, too, made an evaluation: *My babies.*

She drew in another long breath, and came to a second conclusion: *Not food.*

3

Mother's head pulled away to go soaring upward, into the glare of light. First scrambled up the side of the opened nest, into the vast world, followed by her siblings. They frolicked about Mother's huge, rough ankles.

Mother leaned over, opened her mouth, and dropped a glob of viscera onto the ground. The smell ignited First's hunger, a feeling that would accompany her throughout life. She and her siblings devoured their first meal together.

While they feasted, another giant strode near. First inhaled its scent. It was like Mother, and yet different from Mother. *Father.* She looked up and saw Father glaring back at her. Fear rippled through her, but quickly subsided. She was with Mother. She was safe.

First ran and fell, ran and fell, learning to use her body with each passing second. She climbed over Mother's feet and tussled with Second.

Her feelings for Second were a mixture of affection and rivalry. She paid little attention to Third. She liked Last, though, as her brain registered: *No competition.* Last was smaller than her, and a bit slow. She nuzzled him and he made a little cooing noise at her.

First looked upon her world and sucked in the smell of conifers, ferns, water, predators, and prey. Her visual cortex sizzled with new data. Little by little, she made sense of the flood of images: hills, water, plants and other animals. She peered up at Mother, and an ancient part of her brain understood that she was destined to be like her. She lived in a dangerous world, but was meant to be among the mighty rulers of it.

She surveyed her kingdom, let loose with a mighty roar, and promptly tripped over a small twig.

4

Mother and Father left, leaving First and her siblings alone, in the open. First could feel eyes watching her. The broken nest no longer offered protection. There! Something moved behind a cluster of rocks. She hissed a warning at whatever it was and a moment later Second stood by her side to join forces. Third and Last crouched in the remains of the nest.

Now two creatures dashed amidst the rocks, while another closed in from the opposite side. First and Second stood tail-to-tail, hissing. Then, surprisingly, Last joined in while Third burrowed into the soft soil.

One of the creatures sprang to the top of a rock and stood on its strong hind legs, head swaying on a long neck. First, Second and Last all hissed and roared, but that didn't seem to scare it any. It sprang toward them, and the baby allosaurs scattered.

Fear seized First. As much as she may have been hatched into this world to rule, for now she was little more than a snack to most predators. She overcame her fear and kept an eye on this new threat, monitoring and evaluating.

These creatures were fast! One jumped onto a high rock ledge, presumably for a better look at where the chicks were hiding. Again, that head swayed on its snakelike neck. Its legs flexed, ready to make another leap, its eyes fixed on First.

5

The ground shook, and shook again, enough so that this nimble creature lost its foothold and went sliding down the rock. It hit the ground running, though, as Mother let loose with roar that would've been suicide to ignore.

The ornitholestes fled in panic. First added her own roar to hurry them along. One leapt past her only to be snatched out of the air by Mother a second later. Mother bit the birdlike creature in half and let it fall to the ground.

Mother had saved them.

They were safe!

The baby allosaurs ran about in joy. Fear was something felt acutely but also quickly left behind. First stored away the lessons of this ambush for later but didn't let it interfere with the feeling of protection that came from being with Mother.

Something horrible screamed and a moment later one of the ornitholestes was back, and a second after that it had Third clamped in its jaws. First and Second screeched and Mother roared.

Mother bent low, her great jaws wide, but that didn't matter. This creature was already bounding away with the limp, bleeding body of Third in its jaws.

In that moment, the remaining chicks learned their first harsh truth of life: Mother could not always protect them.

6

Mother was restless. She kept stomping off, away from the nest, into the grove of conifers. Then, *stomp, stomp, stomp,* back to the nest. Something was up, but First could not tell what. Were there more of those nasty ornitholestes about? She didn't think that was it.

Then Mother uttered three sharp barking sounds. This was new, but First's body reacted as if poked. Again, Mother stomped off, and this time First found herself, and her siblings, following after.

Mother didn't even turn to make sure they were coming but strode deeper into the nearby conifer forest. Her offspring ran at full speed just to keep up with her long, slow strides.

First cast a look back toward the nest, but it was already out of sight. No matter: it had long since stopped being a source of security. She put it out of her mind and ran ahead of her siblings, determined to maintain her rank as First.

Before long, she smelled water, and a short time later heard a gurgling sound. When they came to the river, the running water caught First's eye. Mother stopped, and First took the opportunity to explore.

A rocky slope led down to the riverbank. First jumped on a rock, not as nimble as the ornitholestes that snatched Third, but not bad. She gave a squeak, expressing a sentiment expressed by the young for countless generations: *Look at me, Ma!*

She jumped to another rock and another, and then Mother did look. First ignored Mother's chuff of exasperation. It wasn't until she was at the water's edge that she peered back up toward Mother.

Her little chest puffed with pride. Certainly this was a feat Mother, with her enormous bulk, could not manage. But instead of approval, Mother only made that barking noise again: a clear command that was not to be disobeyed.

First squeaked again: *Aw, geez, Mom!*

Nevertheless, she dutifully left the river's edge to leapfrog her way back up the rock embankment. The water smelled salty anyway, not good to drink. Midway up, she turned to look longingly back when something enormous and scaly exploded from the water towards her.

Had First frozen in place or ran in panic, things would've turned out badly for the allosaurus chick. But instead, she merely took one quick leap to the next highest rock. The crocodile's long snout landed with a tremendous crash right where First had been a moment before, bringing with it a big rush of water. First almost toppled from the deluge but quickly regained her feet and continued up the slope and out of reach, heart pounding with a mix of fear and excitement.

The crocodile, meanwhile, slid languidly back into the water, unconcerned with this single failure. Except for the occasional explosive lunge, he was a master of energy conservation. This survival strategy served his kind well, through hundreds of millions of years, and multiple extinction events.

First knew nothing of this, of course. She was merely jubilant at having escaped becoming someone's breakfast.

Ha! Too slow, big guy!

First returned to Mother and her siblings. Yes, it had been foolish to leave the relative protection of Mother, but she had gained first-hand experience the others didn't have. If she survived the rest of the day, that experience would come in handy.

Again, Mother began walking, while her chicks struggled to keep up.

7

Mother stopped in a clearing. The ground was damp but the area teemed with insects and small amphibians. First caught on immediately. This was no sightseeing tour. They were here to *hunt*! She lunged at a passing mayfly and missed, but no matter: there were many more. She went after a dragonfly. She didn't get it, but at least felt the wings against her snout.

Following First's lead, Second and Last also chased insects, but their efforts were less vigorous. Maybe they were content to wait until later when Mother would surely give them something tastier. First didn't care about that. She dove for a tiny creature moving about in the mud. It sank down, out of her reach. A moment later, Second bumped against her. First bumped back.

First spotted an exceptionally large dragonfly, but this time she waited. Studied it, watched how it flew. Then she leapt. Her tiny jaws closed upon the insect, and a moment later her hind feet hit the ground, leg muscles absorbing the shock. Already, she was a marvel of biological engineering. Every cell of her small body came alive at that moment.

Nutritionally speaking, the dragonfly was miniscule next to what Mother had provided. But this was the young predator's first kill, and that satisfaction transformed the tiny insect into a wondrous feast.

8

Mother went hunting, leaving the hatchlings alone with Father. There was something off about the way Father moved, and the way he looked at the nestlings filled First with fear. She had always felt uneasy around him, but this time it was worse. His massive stomach rumbled. The nestlings scurried, but there was nowhere safe to go.

Suddenly Father's maw swooped in to fill her world, his rotten-meat breath pushing her off her feet. She wasn't injured, and yet couldn't get back up. Father's mouth opened wide, and still First couldn't move. There only fear and teeth and a looming darkness she couldn't understand.

Then Mother's roar ripped through the wet air. She had returned from her hunt, and was now stomping toward Father. The fear was still on First, but it no longer held her down. First ran. Father lunged for her but Mother was already on him, head tucked low. She rammed Father's underbelly, taking him completely off his feet. He landed hard, setting off a huge gust of wind that sent the nestlings tumbling. They scrambled back to their feet and ran again. Father stayed down, but when he spotted the fleeing babies, his tail lashed out. First went down hard. She got back up, her resilient young body miraculously unhurt.

Mother loomed overhead and roared, long and loud. Father climbed back to his feet and roared back. The two giant carnivores snapped and growled at each other. They stood nose to nose for a long time before Father gave a loud snort and ran off.

9

First, Second and Last trailed after Mother, through the conifers and past the river where First was nearly devoured by a crocodile the day before. They reached an open expanse of dry sand, rock, and nothing else. First's stomach rumbled, but it was more than hunger that drove her today: millions of years of instinct awoke within, instinct that demanded: *Hunt! Kill! Eat! Survive!*

She was not prepared for the vast stretches of time in which nothing happened. She peered way up at Mother's massive head. Mother seemed in no hurry, and in no way inclined to hunt.

A giant, lone sauropod passed, shaking the ground with its slow, careful footfalls, unconcerned with Mother. Mother paid no more attention to this great creature than to the rocks and distant trees. It was too large to bring down, probably even for a pack, and for all practical purposes was nothing but a hill that happened to walk.

They moved on a ways, and then Mother stopped. First looked about, and soon saw what had alerted Mother. Two carnivores strode past, both significantly larger than Mother. One turned his enormous head, opening his maw to reveal long, long teeth. Other than that, the torvosaurs paid no attention to the allosaurus family, and yet their presence revealed to First another harsh lesson of life: her kind was not the biggest, fiercest hunters in this world, as she had thought.

Later, they finally came upon prey animals, and First's heart thudded with excitement. An entire herd of camptosaurs grazed among a copse of conifers. They alternated between moving around on their fours and walking upright. The herd paused at the sight of Mother, but then seemed to sense her disinterest and continued eating. The adult camptosaurs were stocky, yet considerably smaller than Mother, and the babies far smaller still. Mother only looked on impassively. Last gave a squeal of frustration, while Second jumped with excitement.

After what seemed a long time, three bipedal beasts appeared on a ridge, upwind from the campies. They looked similar to the allosaurs, but sported prominent, red horns above their noses and little spikes along their backs. They were mature adults, and yet only about half the size of Mother. Still, they smelled and moved like predators.

First and her siblings drew closer to Mother, but these ceratasaurs had no interest in the allosaurus family.

Instead, they eyed the camptosaurs for a long time without moving or making a sound. It was then that First understood that Mother had brought them here to watch and learn from other hunters. And she was learning, too, though that did little to sate her hunger.

The ceratasaurs, only slightly larger than the prey they stalked, and far outnumbered, began to move. They spread out, seemingly on a silent command from the one female of the group. They stepped with slow, deliberate precision toward the herd, watching for any reaction.

When the reaction came, it was sudden and violent. One campie gave the alarm, a caustic, birdlike shriek that hurt First's tiny ears, and the herd scattered, each member bolting in a different direction. One ran blindly straight toward one of the ceratasaurs, startling the predator almost off his feet. The campie saw its mistake and switched direction with astounding agility for a creature of such weight. The predator hesitated for only a second, but that was enough for the campie to make its escape.

The other male ceratasaur sprinted, and almost brought one down one of the campies, but the prey gave a burst of desperate speed and pulled away from the predator's grasping fore claws.

After mere moments of frenzy, the herd was gone, all except for one baby camptosaurus the female had brought down. Everything had happened so quickly that First completely missed the female ceratasaur's success. The two males came running over, bobbing their heads in submission to their leader.

The female clamped its jaws on her ailing prey, bit down, and ripped out its throat. The aroma of fresh meat and blood wafted over. First's stomach convulsed. She looked to Mother: *Can we hunt now? Can we eat?*

But the lessons had just begun, and the brood still had much to learn.

10

The day went on forever, with long stretches during which nothing happened. Slowly, painfully, First learned patience; perhaps this was the most valuable lesson for a predator.

If patience was the most valuable, safety came in a close second. Prey could be as dangerous as predators, and usually traveled in groups. Plenty of small, relatively defenseless prey animals abounded, but they usually trailed after the giants, such as the armor-plated stegosaurs, for protection.

Every hunt and every ambush brought risk. First watched as a juvenile allosaurus charged a small ornithopod that had mistakenly wandered off by itself. It should have been an easy kill, but the juvenile rushed and lost his footing at the last second. He tripped over a large rock and went down hard. The ornithopod moved slowly but steadily away.

Mother eyed the creature, and First thought this would be it, this would be their meal. Instead, she turned away and led her brood on. First began to wonder if she would ever eat again. The Sun began edging toward the horizon, and Mother had shown almost no interest in hunting. To make matters worse, the smell of meat and blood again drifted to her nostrils.

Mother led them toward the aroma. Soon they had to run to keep up. First's legs began to feel like hollow twigs as hunger, exhaustion, and now thirst took their toll. She hoped Mother would slow soon, but instead her strides only grew longer and faster. First and her two siblings squealed in frustration and fear as they fell steadily behind.

The blood smell grew stronger, making First almost crazy with hunger. Mother strode nearly out of sight as the Sun touched the horizon. First was sure she would starve, or get eaten now that Mother was no longer towering over her. She ran, almost blindly, unsteady on her feet, and too winded to cry out.

Her fear grew as a new terror emerged: the shadows of a flock of pterosaurs soaring overhead. Pterosaurs had never presented a threat in themselves but she had seen how these tiny scavengers appeared whenever something had died or was about to die. Now it seemed they were waiting for the time when she would fall and not rise again. Fear pulsed through the tissues of her young body.

She wanted to rest. She wanted to lie down and give up, but she would not give the pterosaurs that satisfaction. The winged pests annoyed her. She refused to be their next meal.

Second and Last stumbled along behind. First stopped and turned. Second caught up readily, and then Last came along, tripping and falling and getting up again. First felt affection for her two siblings, especially Last. But she was also hungry. How difficult would it be to jump Last, catching him off guard? Would Second try to stop her? Or would she help?

Maybe this was the real lesson for today: to survive by any means possible. She was close, very close, to going after Last when Mother's sharp, commanding bark ripped through the air.

Their bodies responded automatically. They looked toward Mother and began running with new vigor. Mother waited until they caught up. Just ahead, two juvenile allosaururs and several pterosaurs feasted on the downed carcass of a baby apatasaurus.

First, Second, and Last finally caught up, and the family advanced on the carcass. The two juveniles stopped eating to face them. They snarled and shifted their weight from foot to foot, but Mother was not to be intimidated. She let forth with a loud, long roar that scattered the juveniles. Most of the pterosaurs took wing, but one remained behind. First dashed up and roared at it. It flew off.

So this was how it was done!

Mother tore into the carcass and pulled forth a huge chunk of soft meat, which she tossed down for her brood to feast upon. First had done her share, scaring off the pterosaur, and so bit into the well-earned, fresh meat with pride.

After gorging themselves, the family bedded down near the carcass. Mother opened her mouth, and a small pterosaur swooped in to pick the meat from between her teeth. First opened her own mouth, and soon the pterosaur performed the same service for her.

Usually, she hated these winged pests, but this one was okay.

11

Over the next few weeks, Mother took her brood on ever-longer expeditions. They had left the nest behind and took to bedding down wherever they could find a patch of soft ground.

First learned more and more every day, soaking up lessons like a dry sponge soaks up water. She learned that patience was the key to success. With prey animals traveling in herds or trailing after giants for protection, they often had to wait for a straggler to emerge. It took patience to wait for the right opportunity and the right moment. First and her siblings watched many predators as they stalked and waited and attacked.

Sometimes the predators succeeded, but more often the prey was too swift or too lucky. Sometimes the predators were hurt worse than the prey. She watched a juvenile allosaurus rush a full-grown stegosaurus that had wandered from its herd. The stegosaurus, a stupid but deadly animal, became aware of the threat only when the juvenile was nearly upon it, but that was time enough. Its spiked tail lashed out and caught the predator square in the thigh. The inept hunter went down hard, while the stegosaurus went on its way without a scratch.

Her first hard truth of life was that Mother could not always protect her. Then she learned that her kind were not the mightiest in the world. Now she learned more harsh truths. Any hunt could lead to injury. An injured predator is a poor hunter. Injury can lead to death.

First and her siblings grew quickly. Sometimes Mother wouldn't bring them food, and so they would be driven to hunt lizards and dig up the various strange, furry creatures that burrowed underground. One time, First charged an archaeopteryx. It dashed off, and even started to fly, in a clumsy fashion, but First grappled it to the ground. It lashed out, its sharp, middle toe nicking First's chest. It was a small cut but drew blood. It was the first time the young allosaurus had bled, and the smell drove her into a frenzy. She shook the bird viciously, tore it apart, and devoured it. Second approached, but when First shrieked, her sibling backed away.

After First had grown to the height of Mother's knee, she attacked a stranded baby gargoyleosaurus. Even though it was infant, its bony armor and spikes were impossible to tear through. What's more, even though slow, it was heavier than First.

First wasn't about to give up. She jumped on its back and tried to bite into its neck. No luck, as that was as armored as every other part. Mother stepped over, but First hissed at her. She actually hissed at Mother! She went back to wrestling with the armored creature, and finally succeeded in tipping it to one side. It struggled, but fell over. First wasted no time but, dodging its flailing legs, tore into the soft belly. Last also took a bite while Second tore out the creature's throat.

The three of them feasted on their first group kill while Mother stood by.

12

One day Mother led them to within sight of a massive stegosaurus. Unlike most of its kind, this one kept to itself, chasing away small prey animals that sought its protection. It finished grazing and climbed to the top of a rock formation. This was a perfect defensive position, as one side of the formation was a sheer drop and impossible to attack from. From this vantage, it snarled at all that passed, its tail flaring red at the least provocation.

A full-grown torvosaurus passed by, and the stegosaurus grunted and charged, running down the sloped side of the formation. The giant prey animal chased off the startled predator.

From a safe distance, First turned and roared at the stegosaurus. The stego grunted, and whipped its spiked tail in her direction.

13

Mother's final lesson in patience came on the day she led her offspring onto the salt flats. The flats stretched out forever, and First could see no reason for entering the desolate expanse of arid land. Still, Mother led them on and on.

Without trees or ridges for protection, the sun blazed, threatening to blister their skin. Thirst soon overpowered hunger as First, Second and Last trailed behind Mother on an endless trek.

They came upon a vast diplodocus herd. The sauropods plodded along their migration route, paying scant attention to Mother and her brood. From everything First had seen, attacking one of these behemoths would have been suicide. Still, Mother followed them, albeit from a distance. On one of their journeys, First had seen a diplodocus lash out with its tail at a ceratasaurus that gotten too close. The foolish predator hit the ground hard, and only rose again long after the diplodocus had passed from sight.

The key was patience.

Patience.

Waiting.

First followed Mother's gaze. One of the baby diplodocuses was limping. It trailed near the back of the herd, bleating continually, but none of the adults paid it much mind.

Its limp grew worse, but it fought to stay within the safety of the group. It kept pace for a long time, despite its obvious injury.

The salt flats went on and on until First could see nothing besides the heat haze rising from the ground. Trees, lakes, and rivers were nothing but a memory now. First was beginning to wonder if this expedition would end in failure. She had certainly seen plenty of failed kills in her short life.

One bad stumble sent the baby diplodocus to the ground. She rose again, but slowly. When she was finally back on her feet, the last of the herd was passing by. She ran to catch up, only to fall again. She struggled to her feet, and stood wobbling, while the herd moved on without her.

Mother approached and the diplodocus bleated louder than ever. It tried to turn its tail toward Mother but could barely move. Mother closed in, chomped down once on the base of the baby's neck, and backed away.

The bite was not immediately fatal, but it did make the baby bleed profusely, even as it tried desperately to regain the herd. First felt a mixture of pity and hunger. But mostly hunger.

They waited a long, long time for exhaustion, thirst, and injury to overtake the baby diplodocus. When Mother finally delivered the fatal bite, it was a mercy killing.

This was Mother's most difficult hunting lesson for her young allosaurs. It was also the last.

14

The next day, they returned to the conifer forest.

While First and her siblings rested, trying to regain their strength after the arduous journey across the salt flats, Mother leaned over them, her great head looming close. The giant female sucked a long breath through her nostrils. Then a wave of hot, meaty wind flew from her mouth, followed by another long in-breath.

Something was wrong.

Something was different. Something had changed.

Mother made a sound deep in her throat and reared back so quickly it scared First. She sensed something off about the way Mother moved, and the way she looked at her brood.

Mother growled, softly at first, but the sound quickly erupted into a terrible roar. It was not the first time she had heard her mother roar like this, but never before had it been directed at her young, as this most certainly was.

Compelled by sheer, survival instinct, First ran from Mother. Second and Last also bolted, but First quickly outpaced them. Later, after exhaustion eventually forced her to stop, her siblings were nowhere in sight. She would never see them again, except in dreams.

Earlier that morning, her fear had started to recede as her rule of this world began to bloom, even if there were larger predators about. But now her newfound confidence, in herself and in the world, vanished like dew in sunshine.

Her mother, her protector, had become something to fear. Now, for the first time in her existence, she was on her own.

She stopped running and surveyed her world with new eyes. Her mother was no longer in sight, and that was a relief. She set off for the horizon, as alert and skittish as a hatchling.

Large shapes moved in the distance. Emotions stirred in her brain and tingled through her body. A sense of loss, to be sure, but something else moved in her as well. She had no word for this alien emotion, but if she had, if would've been freedom.

15

For several days after Mother left, First set out hunting but made no kill. Many lizards skittered by. Some were easy targets, and yet she hesitated, and they escaped. On the third day her hunger reached a peak, her stomach became a painful rock, and her thinking began to cloud. She spent most of the daylight hours stalking a herd of stegosaurs. The stegos were large, slow, stupid, and dangerous. First was far from full-grown. Trying to bring down one of these stegosaurs would've been suicide. Nevertheless, they caught her attention, and she could not pull herself away.

She wanted to find a baby straggler but had no such luck: they all seemed remarkably strong and healthy. Sunset came, cooling the air. Her metabolism slowed but the driving hunger raged on, and she kept her eye on the stegos as they lumbered into a vast plain of sawgrass to graze and bed down. Over the course of the day she had moved in closer to the herd. Their initial skittishness over having a predator nearby had long since abated.

The herd settled in for the night, the solid beasts lowering their bodies to the ground, close and sometimes touching each other, for protection and warmth.

First stood less than a body's length from the nearest one. The desire to sleep started to overcome her, and yet food was so very close. Saliva absolutely poured from her mouth, and her stomach clenched in agonizing spasms. Three days without food, for a growing allosaurus, felt like a lifetime.

Her pupils dilated as dark drew on, bringing the herd into sharp focus. The smell of prey nearly drove her mad with hunger. And yet, the herd had settled in for the night, no longer concerned with her presence. As hungry as she was, it would have been suicide to attack any member of this healthy, robust herd. As slow and stupid as the stegosaurs were, they knew this as well as she.

She stood that way, nearly touching one of the stegosaurs, until sleep finally overtook her, and she lowered herself to the soft, grassy ground a mere tail length from the nearest stegosaurus.

16

The rain began soon after she fell asleep. She shivered through the night, burning precious reserves of energy. When dawn came, marked only by a dim appearance of Sun, the herd was gone, and the rain showed no sign of stopping. Getting to her feet was a struggle: the downpour had made the grass slippery, and her cold muscles ached.

Born during the dry season, First had never known a rain like this. The rainy season had just begun, and she did not like it one bit.

Still, she had to go on. She had to find food. She began her morning trek carefully, digging her talons into the ground as she went. What she had gained in bulk and strength, she had lost in agility. As she had seen during her journeys with Mother, a single fall could lead to severe injury, and an injury could lead to death.

On top cold, hunger, and soreness, First missed Mother.

The herd of stegosaururs returned and tromped by. They were steady and sure-footed on the wet ground but seemed miserable nonetheless. They paid First no attention whatsoever.

She drew a long breath through her nose, smelling for even the slightest tinge of prey. She had to find something smaller than stegosaurs. No such luck. As the day wore on, things did not improve. The rain paused briefly, only to come down with renewed vigor a short time later. The ground became drenched, and streams formed everywhere she walked. She could not stop shivering, nor could she find any real shelter from the blowing, slanting downpour. The Sun, a blurry ball of light, offered little comfort.

She came upon the ornitholestes completely by surprise: her surprise as well as the ornitholestes'. It was alone and curled into a tight ball, trying to keep warm in the chill air. It spotted First, gave a little cry, and scrambled to its feet.

First's jaws came down on its head even before she made a conscious decision to attack. She began to devour her kill, then stopped. She dropped the mangled body on the rain-soaked ground to get a good look at it.

It was the same kind of creature that had terrorized First and her siblings in the nest. The same kind that had run off with Third's body in its jaws.

In that moment, she regained something that she had no word for and did not realize she had lost: her confidence. She knew then she would survive. She would grow bigger and stronger. She would be among the rulers of this harsh world.

She was First!

She was the one who would've devoured her own favorite sibling rather than perish.

She was First!

Thunder boomed and lightning tore across the sky, but First roared in rage and defiance right back at it.

17

First adapted to the rainy season, but still hated it. Hunting was treacherous, so she exercised her hard-learned patience and waited for opportunity to come to her. Sometimes it did. Other times she resorted to digging up furry creatures from the soft, drenched ground.

Nights were the worst. Usually she shivered her way through the darkness, sleeping fitfully, and rarely falling into deep slumber. One night she sought refuge in a small cave, only to awaken later in rising floodwater. Wherever she went, the rain found her and made her miserable.

Poor sleep slowed her reactions during the day, making every hunt all the more risky. Fortunately, many prey animals seemed to be even more dim-witted and sluggish than usual. She fed but never quite enough to satisfy her growing needs.

By the time the rains tapered off, and the Sun once again shone bright, First was ravenous. The ground was still drenched, but at least the days were warmer. She took to napping on her feet, leaning against a rock ledge and soaking up the sunshine. The heat was almost better than food, and it lifted her spirits.

She had rarely seen other predators during the rains, but now occasionally caught sight of a pair of her own kind, a male and a female. They were about her age but slightly smaller. Then, during one of her daytime naps, they approached.

First snapped out of her doze to face this new threat. Only they weren't threatening but bobbing their heads in submission to her. They didn't want to fight. Though smaller than First, they could probably defeat her by working together. But they would both sustain injuries themselves and, as First had learned, injury can lead to death.

No, they clearly wanted something else.

They wanted her for their pack. First almost drove them off then but thought better of it. She was growing rapidly and so was her appetite. The small prey she had been feeding on would not sustain her much longer.

She approached and their head bobbing increased. The female had a big splotch of white on her face, while the male had a long, healed-over gash running down his chest. Splotch and Gash recognized her as an alpha, but just to make sure, First roared. They ran off a ways, stopped, and returned. They bobbed their heads at her. It was clear they had accepted her as their leader and were glad to have her in the pack.

First was also pleased, albeit a bit wary. *Let's just see how they work out.* It was past time to go on a real hunt. First raised her head high and gave two commanding barks, then turned to set off at a brisk pace. She did not look back, nor did she have to.

She knew they would follow.

18

First needed a good hunt to both prove her own abilities and to test her new troops. Still, it would not be sensible to take an unnecessary risk. The three were still far from full-grown, so hunting any of the giants was beyond the ability of their little pack. Besides, she had learned that patience was often rewarded with opportunity.

First led her troops past stegosaurs and various sauropods. She studied a group of ceratasaurs, but they all seemed fit enough, no stragglers.

Splotch and Gash began to snap at each other, but not at their new leader. She could have led them back to the ceratasaurs in hopes that a baby might wander off by itself, but her experience told her that wasn't the way.

The day wore on and several times she had to turn and give reprimanding barks when the fighting of her followers grew serious. She knew they must be hungry. She certainly was.

But she was also patient.

It wasn't until almost sunset that her patience was rewarded, but the reward was worth it. A short ways into a conifer forest they came upon a large, wounded predator. It was like the ones she had seen before, larger than Mother or any other of their kind. This one had apparently tripped, most likely while pursuing prey. He lay in the mud snarling at First and her crew. One leg was badly broken, with the bone poking far out of the flesh. He studied them with glazed eyes and seemed to have trouble keeping his head up.

Even though seriously wounded, this full-grown torvosaurus was dangerous. First studied him while her troops looked to her for guidance.

This was a new situation, but First knew she could not appear weak or indecisive. She was the leader. She was First. She barked a command: *Stay back!* Then she moved carefully around the wounded predator, watching out for its lashing tail. The torvosaur tried to roll over to face her, but exhaustion had clearly taken its toll.

First crept up behind, reached over, and ripped one razor sharp fore claw across the larger animal's neck. She dug deep and brought forth a good fount of blood. The torvosaur, enraged as well as scared now, finally managed to roll over, but First backed away, out of reach.

She gave another commanding bark, this one directed at Splotch. The female closed in on the torvosaur from the other side and slashed his belly, and backed away. The Torvosaur was not able to roll over again. First barked at Gash, who moved in, slashed the neck, and stepped back.

First stalked off a ways and commanded her underlings to come to her. They came, and stood by her side watching the carnivore thrash and bleed. There was no sense in inflicting further injury, as every contact brought new risk.

As with so many times in the past, patience was the key. They stood guard as the sun slipped beneath the horizon. It was full dark when the torvosaur finally bled out, but they were lucky, and no other predators came to claim the prize.

The new pack feasted under a blood-red moon.

19

First, Splotch and Gash went on to make many successful kills together. One reason for the pack's success was that neither Splotch nor Gash had any interest in challenging First for the position of pack leader. As long as First performed her role and they stayed fed, there was no reason to change anything.

Another reason was First's patience. She was willing to wait for opportunity and willing to pass up risky situations for something better. This was a trait she taught her troops, by example, and it paid off.

One of First's favorite hunting grounds was the thick grasses near rivers and the inland sea. She often stalked, heron-like, through the wetlands in search of young crocodiles.

Even a small crocodile can be fast and deadly, but First was more cunning. And, with Splotch and Gash backing her up, deadlier. Her technique was to catch a slumbering croc by surprise, roll it onto its back, and then give the command for her troops to charge in and attack the belly. After that, it was a matter of standing back while the reptile bled out.

The lessons of their first kill, that of the full-grown torvosaurus, served the trio well. Over the next four years, fed by numerous successful hunts, they grew larger, stronger, more skilled, and far more fearsome.

First grew the most. As they edged toward adolescence, she stood a head taller than both. With her at the lead, they sometimes fed without having to hunt at all. That was a matter of driving off other juvenile predators from their own kills. Feasting on carrion involved less risk than hunting, and meat was meat, however it was attained.

The day came when they came upon an adult allosaurus devouring a baby stegosaurus. First approached cautiously and sniffed.

It was Mother!

Her mother looked up from the carcass and her lips pulled back. Splotch and Gash stood by waiting for orders to retreat. That would be the smart thing.

That order never came. Instead, First directed her well-trained troops to spread out. They hesitated only momentarily before complying. Now First's mother looked at each in turn before returning her gaze upon First.

First stood her ground even as her mother charged. Splotch and Gash moved in from both sides. The aged adult stopped in her tracks and turned toward Splotch. First moved in, slashed her mother across the chest, and dashed off. It was far from a fatal wound but had gone deep enough to draw blood.

They faced each other a long time. Eventually, Mother bobbed her head once and stalked off to find her supper elsewhere. First watched her disappear over the horizon, her heartbeat thumping loud in her ears.

After that victory, First began to play with the idea of going after larger prey. Something like a grown stegosaurus entailed considerable risk, but no more so than the many smaller risks they routinely took on to get the same amount of meat. And now they were feared enough that they could defend such a kill, even against an adult.

Meat was meat, but there was also the pride of a fine kill. First vaguely recalled the immense satisfaction she had as a chick, feasting on the dragonfly she had killed herself.

It was a warm night when she bedded down on the soft ground of the conifer forest and decided it was time to start going after bigger game. She would still be patient and wait for opportunity. She would do right by her troops. But her heart pounded with anticipation of the glorious hunts.

First looked over at Splotch and Gash, lying close together, sharing body heat. She felt affection and respect for them. She would take them on a successful hunt for bigger prey. She would take them out upon the salt flats, as her mother had taken her so long ago. They would bring down a sauropod. Her troops would feast for days and glory in her leadership.

She drifted into a pleasant slumber, not knowing that the next harsh truth of life awaited her.

And it would find her very soon.

20

It was a lazy morning for the three young allosaurs. They awoke in the sunshine that streamed through the trees and basked in the warmth. Splotch and Gash rose to their feet, yawned and bumped against each other playfully. First looked on, still lying on the ground, enjoying the sun. Her troops were fine, healthy young predators. Gash had proved his cunning on many occasions. Perhaps he would be a suitable mate in the future. Of course, First would have to drive off Splotch before that could happen, but she didn't see any problem there.

And yet, all that lay only in a hazy future, and First had patience enough to wait. She rolled to her feet and roared out a yawn. Splotch and Gash jumped, then bumped against each other again. It was a fine morning, and everyone was warm and only slightly hungry.

First set out. She gave no command, as they were far past that. Splotch and Gash followed along, ready for whatever their trusted leader had in store.

When they reached the salt flats, First almost turned back. She sucked in a long breath through her nostrils and detected nothing from the barren expanse of dry, cracked land. It was turning into a blistering day, and the ground burned her feet.

Nevertheless, this was the path she had chosen, and she wasn't about to turn away. Not with her loyal troops following. The sun baked their hides after only a short trek into the flats. Heat haze closed off the rest of the world, and before long her troops' playfulness gave way to irritation. They snapped at each other, which they had not done for a long time.

Patience. That was the key. Even as she could still detect no prey scent by mid-day, determination boiled in her blood. Unfortunately, hours of sweating with nothing to drink sapped her strength and, with it, her confidence. She still had zero sign of prey and questionable reserves of energy to hunt even if they did find something.

After another hour, First knew the expedition was a bust. Worse, was dizzy and too disoriented to know the way back to the conifers. Worse yet, Splotch and Gash were now turning their frustrated growls toward her.

Her two followers, accomplished fighters by now, could probably take her down if they teamed up. But even if they couldn't, any battle out in this desolate land would likely end in doom.

There would be zero survival advantage in them attacking, but their tempers and desperation could easily overpower good sense.

First was bigger and stronger. And faster. She picked up her pace, even as her stomach clenched from thirst, and her legs wanted nothing but rest. She had faced down hunger, thirst, and exhaustion before. They would not defeat her now.

She began to run at a moderate pace. If nothing else, she would make sure that Splotch and Gash would simply be too tired to form an attack.

Then she smelled something. Not prey, but perhaps something even better: water. Her strides grew longer as she loped swiftly toward the aroma.

Eventually, parched ground slowly gave way to grasses and ferns. Further on, they came to a freshwater river. They stopped and drank deeply. First sniffed the air and this time caught the smell of saltwater.

Saltwater meant crocodiles.

She led them upriver, toward the smell of brine. She had never been to this area before but had seen enough rivers and wetlands to know what to expect. There was hope for a kill yet. But first, they needed to get closer to the sea.

They came to the shore of the great, inland sea at last. They stood panting. Gash spotted something in the water. While he watched it, Splotch came up and playfully bumped against him. He bumped her back. Their good mood was restored, at least for the moment.

First peered on. They were watching a school of large fish that swam in the deep water of a drop-off. Gash slipped on the muddy bank and had to scramble to keep from plunging in. If a dinosaur could laugh, First and Splotch would've at that moment.

At least they no longer seemed inclined to team up against her. The salt flats expedition was a failure, but such setbacks were to be expected. Patience was often, but not always, rewarded.

First stalked off in search of crocodiles. She was able to roll full-grown crocs now, so long as she caught them by surprise. She'd find one and make up for—

A long, high-pitched sound like nothing she had ever heard before ripped through the air. She whipped her head around to see what was happening.

Gash and Splotch were shrieking in alarm.

21

First beheld a sight that would haunt her the rest of her life. An impossibly large mouth exploded from the deep water, bringing with it a wave that hit Splotch and Gash almost hard enough to take them off their feet.

First stood frozen as the great jaws opened. Long teeth glinted in the setting Sun. Splotch and Gash stood shrieking. The jaws rotated in the water. Splotch finally began to move, but it was too late, as the jaws closed upon her, enveloping her head and upper body both. First shrieked, and Gash shrieked, but all that was drowned out by the crashing of the water.

The beast flipped Splotch's kicking legs off the ground for a second that went on forever, and then dragged her under the deep water.

First felt her senses overload. She stood staring at the place where Splotch had just been. She moved barely in time to avoid being rammed by Gash, running blind and wild. She turned and barked a warning, but it did no good. Gash tripped on a branch and went down hard, his head smacking a rock. Then he lay sprawled and curiously silent, with only the sound of air rushing through his nostrils. His neck was bent at a sharp angle. He watched First with wide, unblinking eyes.

First stood by as Gash slowly died. A light rain fell. First had been a good leader for the last few years because she usually knew what to do. She could make decisions and stand by them. Now she had no idea what to do, nor could she understand what had happened. Only a few minutes ago she was hunting crocodiles while her troops watched fish and flirted with each other.

The drizzle gave way to a heavy torrent. Once again, the rainy season began as it often had before: quickly and without warning.

First knew it would be best to give Gash a quick, merciful death. But she could not bring herself to rip out the throat of the one she had earlier considered as a future mate. Instead, she stalked about, back and forth, as the life slowly drained from his broken body.

Just the night before, First had a pack, a good life, and hopes for the future. She had big plans for them all. Now she stood in the rain as another harsh truth of life sank in: Everything could be taken away at a moment's notice.

She tilted her head and opened her mouth, but it wasn't a roar of defiance that emerged this time. Instead, it was a new sound: a long, long wail of mourning.

22

They appeared like ghosts out of the downpour: five torvosaurs, two of them adults and the rest nearly full-grown. Each was considerably bulkier than First.

They were here for the carcass of Gash and nothing more. First saw a clear escape route. She could flee and there would be no survival advantage for them to give chase, just as there was no sense for First to stay.

First snarled and charged right for the largest torvosaur. She had no plan whatsoever. She was angry and confused, and she had to take it out on something. Maybe the senselessness of the charge was what startled the adult torvosaur, but whatever it was he sidestepped awkwardly to get out of her way. First bumped into him on the way past, knocking the larger predator to the ground.

First kept running. Between the thunder and heavy rain, she could not tell if the torvosaurs were giving chase or whether they let her go. It didn't matter. She ran for a long time. It takes lots of energy to run in the mud: every footfall has to be placed carefully. She didn't care. She ran herself to exhaustion, and with no regard for where she was headed.

Another rainy season had set in, and First was alone.

23

Instinct, hunger, and a stubborn spirit drove First to survive another rainy season. She ate a lot of crocodiles. Crocs might be one of the most successful species ever, but First savored each short-term victory over the reptile.

One morning she followed something. She couldn't tell what it was in the driving rain, but it led her onto the salt flats. Before long, she lost sight of it. The flats began to flood, the water rising over her feet. She thought she saw something move in the water, and then she was sure the giant sea creature was going to break from the floodwater to drag her down. She ran and didn't stop until she was on the other side of the flats.

She spent the rest of the rainy season back in familiar territory. When the rains finally stopped, and the sun shone bright, she once again took to napping against her favorite rock ledge. Later, she came across the same lone stegosaurus she had known so long ago. The stego was ancient by now but every bit as mean-spirited as ever, defending its territory atop the rock formation.

First felt both happy and sad at the sight of the old stegosaurus. She thought of the time Mother had first brought her this way. She had growled at the giant stego, albeit from a safe distance.

Had all that really happened? She had been so small back then, the world so huge and new. Life had shown her much since, both good and bad. Maybe it would be nice to raise a family of her own, and introduce a new generation to the wonders of this world.

Her stomach rumbled. It was time to start looking for opportunity again. Very soon, an opportunity of a different sort approached. He came toward her with head bobbing, not so much in submission but to show he was no threat. He was a young adult, the same as First, and a fine specimen at that. A limp archaeopteryx hung from his jaws. He bobbed his way toward her and gently placed the offering on the ground.

Bob, bob, bob.

First approached and sniffed the kill. It was hardly even a snack, but it was the gesture that counted. It said, *I could hunt while you tend the nest.*

First roared and charged. It was not a big roar, but the male got the message. He ran off. Stopped and turned. First roared again, and he traipsed off.

It would be good to have a mate and raise a family, but not yet.

Someday.

24

First awoke in sunshine. She rolled onto her back and let the rays warm her belly. She was in a good mood. She had slept well, with no sea-creature nightmares. Now she flipped to her feet and surveyed her kingdom. Full-grown now, she was not the largest predator about, but bigger than any others of her own kind. And she was patient and cunning. In a way, she had mastered this world, just as she always suspected she would.

She set out on her morning trek and roared at the giant, aged stegosaurus, standing atop his rock formation. The stego grumbled at her. It thrashed its spiked tail. First roared. The stego grumbled and thrashed. This went on for a time. It was a fun game, and many creatures stopped what they were doing to watch.

First moved on, leaving the grumbly stegosaurus to his rock pile. Something inside her sensed that this was her day, and she had better enjoy it because another like it might never come along.

She found a waterfall under a cliff ledge and stood beneath it. The water was cold, almost painfully so, but it also felt good and made her alert.

Later, she lay sprawled on the ground, soaking up sunshine. It felt incredibly good after the cold shower. She lay very still, and before long a band of ornithostholes scurried by. Those nasty little lizards, like the one that stole her nestling so long ago.

The lizards realized their mistake too late. She snatched one with her fore claws and broke its neck. She got to her feet and held the pathetic little creature. It wasn't even worth eating. Instead, she dropped it on the ground, strode off a ways, and looked on as it was devoured by its own kind.

It crossed her mind to hunt, but only briefly. This was her day, and opportunity would emerge. She was patient. She surveyed the activity of her world. A mother allosaurus passed by with four chicks trailing after. An over-eager young ceratasaurus tried to ambush a camptosaurus and failed miserably. Only by sheer luck did he get away without being trampled by the herd.

She settled down for a nap, stretching and yawning luxuriously. She came as close to a feeling of gratitude as a carnivorous dinosaur is capable. After drifting off to sleep, a tiny pterosaur landed in her open mouth, looking for scraps of meat. First woke, spied the pterosaur, and slammed her mouth shut on it. Then she came as close to laughter as ever a carnivorous dinosaur is capable.

Near the day's end, First again wandered over to within sight of the big stegosaurus. Then, starting from a long ways off, she charged, shrieking as she went. The stego turned and thrashed his tail spikes. He turned again and growled.

Thrash! Thrash! Thrash!

One back foot slipped over the ledge of his rock formation. He bellowed defiance and tried to regain his footing, but his weight was too great. First stopped just short of the rocks and watched as the huge, ornery old stegosaur lost his fight with gravity to tumble backwards over the ledge, onto his own armor plates. A tremendous sound of breakage erupted from behind the rock.

By the time First stalked around, the great beast was still. She approached, for once foregoing her usual patience. In the moment before its death, the stegosaurus thrashed his spiked tail into First's side, taking her completely off her feet.

First hit the ground hard, and everything went dark.

25

First dreamt.

In her dream, she had a family. She dug her little ones out of the nest and inhaled their scent, very much as her own mother had inhaled hers, so long ago.

She let her babies tussle with each other and run across her feet and hide behind her legs. It gave her joy to watch them.

Her mate stood nearby. Last season, he had returned to court her again. This time he placed an ornithostholes at her feet, and she knew he was the right male for her.

Presently, she gave him a little roar of warning when he looked at the chicks with a gleam of menace in his eye. Then she gazed upon her brood and uttered a brand new sound, a gentle cooing that said she would always protect her babies. The song carried all the love and all the promises of which an allosaurus is capable.

Then pain exploded inside her mouth, and the song turned to a shriek. The agony in her jaw spread, spiking through her head like fissures in a rock. Everything went dark, as if she had shut her eyes at night.

When her sight returned, the pain had abated. She stood panting, her sides heaving. Only after a long time did she notice that one of her babies hung limp and bloody from her mouth.

26

Morning broke and still she dreamt, even as she lay half awake. Now it was the giant sea creature swimming through her mind. Everywhere she went, the gargantuan mouth rose from the sea or from the ground. It pushed up from the parched and cracking floor of the salt flats to chomp on her legs. It emerged from the ground of the conifer forest to swallow her whole.

She was on her feet even before fully awake. The dream lingered in her brain like a parasite, and the sun hurt her eyes. Something small ran past, and she jumped so much as to almost lose her footing.

She searched around for Splotch and Gash. They would help her. She would lead them in a hunt for whatever was hurting her. Maybe Mother would join the hunt, and then they would be unstoppable.

Something started biting her jaw. She rubbed her mouth on a tree, but whatever was gnawing on her hung on. She'd have to find Mother. She would help.

Some ways off, a massive stegosaurus carcass baked in the sun. A pterosaur picked at its open skull, but otherwise it was left alone. She vaguely remembered tearing into it the night before.

Why were no other scavengers feasting on it? Maybe they were afraid of Mother. Yes. Mother must be nearby, guarding the kill, scaring off carrion eaters.

First stalked over and sniffed. The meat smelled odd, but if Mother was watching, everything had to be okay. Mother always protected her. Where was Mother now? She was probably behind that big rock.

First feasted on the stegosaur. It tasted funny at first, but she soon stopped noticing and just ate. After consuming her fill, she climbed onto the rock formation. Heated by the morning sun, the rock blistered her feet but she didn't mind. From here, she could keep watch for Mother and Second and Third and Last. It had been a long time since she had seen her nestlings, and she missed them.

And where were Splotch and Gash? When they returned, she would lead them on a glorious hunt. They would bring down grown stegosaurs and sauropods. Then she would drive off Splotch, mate with Gash, and bring forth a new generation of mighty hunters.

She was First!

Her rule would always last.

Standing tall on her rock, she bellowed a great roar, and surveyed her kingdom.

Made in the USA
Middletown, DE
07 September 2019